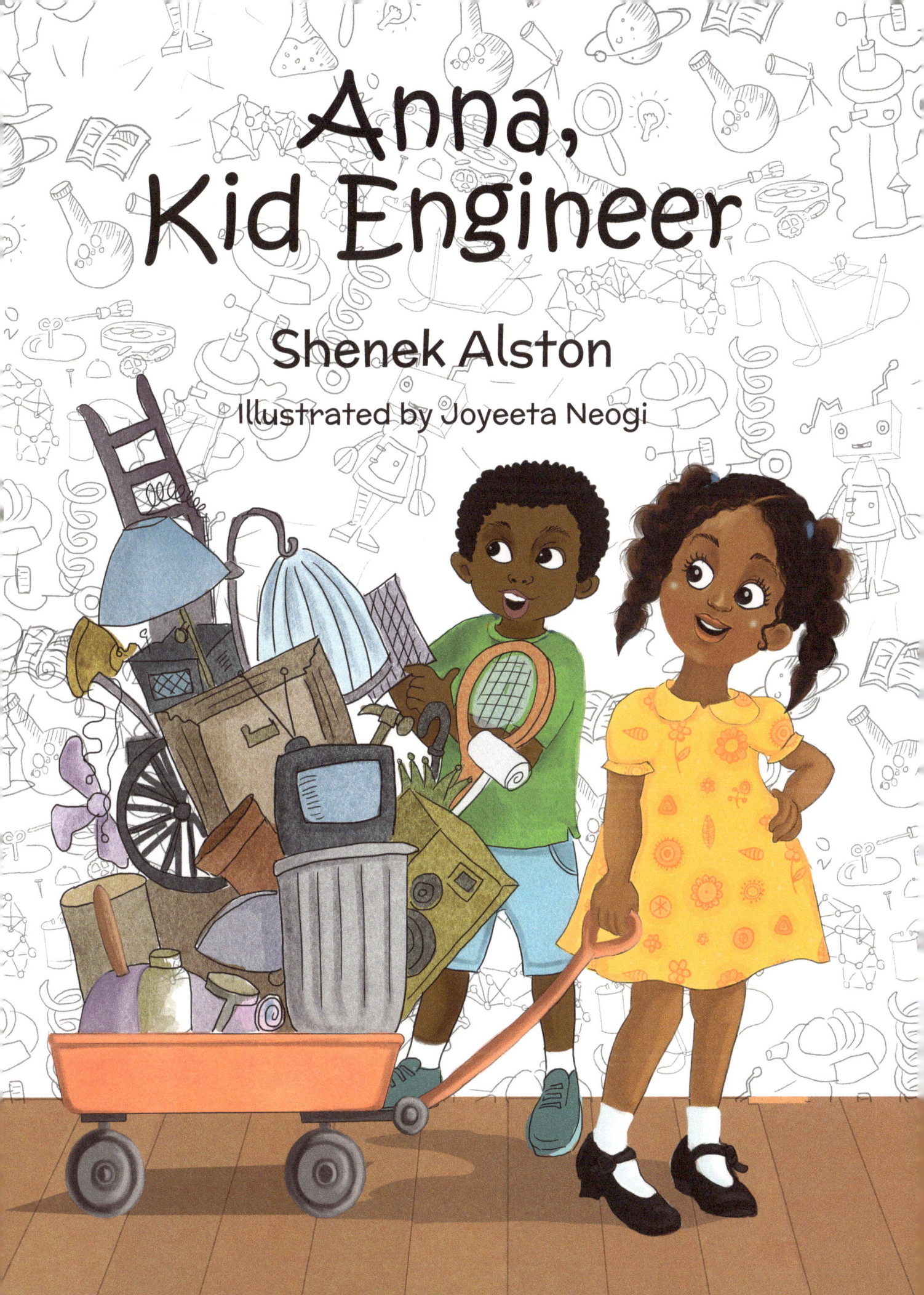

Copyright © 2018 Shenek Alston

ISBN: 978-0-692-08159-4

All rights reserved, including the right to reproduce this book or portions thereof in any form whatsoever. Apart from any fair dealing for the purpose of research or private study, or criticism or review, no part of this publication may be reproduced, stored in or introduced into a retrieval system, or transmitted, in any form or by any means (electronic, mechanical, photocopying, recording or otherwise), without the prior written permission of the copyright owner.

www.annakidengineer.com

To God – To Whom All Praises Are Owed

To André, my husband – For loving me

To Annaliese, André, and Abigail,
my three little cups whom I love dearly

To Dad and Mom – For always loving me

It was that time of the year again: the annual Science Fair at East Creek Elementary School was in 5 weeks. Anna was in 5th grade this year and wanted to have an awesome project, especially since this was her last year of elementary school.

The last 2 years, she had the hardest time coming up with a good project. She thought back on her 3rd-grade project: an erupting volcano like many other kids had. Oh, how embarrassing that was, and her volcano didn't even erupt that high! Then her 4th-grade project wasn't much better. But this year was going to be different, or was it?

"Hey, Anna, the Science Fair is in 5 weeks. I'll never forget that year when a bunch of us did those volcanoes. I guess no one will ever forget since they put a picture of us in the newspaper. The adults thought it was so cute, but we sure didn't think it was cute," her friend Joshua said.

Joshua was in the same line-up with the other kids with the volcano project a couple of years ago.

"I know they say that great minds think alike, but that year with the volcanoes was just RIDICULOUS," Joshua said.

"Nah, no great ideas yet," I sighed.

"Hey, don't be discouraged. You love tinkering and creating new things. I know you can come up with an awesome idea," Joshua said.

"Are you entering this year?" I asked Joshua.

"No, Mom said that I have enough on my plate already, and that if I can't put my best foot forward that I shouldn't enter it. But I'll be there rooting you on," Joshua said as he smiled.

"Thanks, Joshua, I know that you will," I said as we were about to part ways to head to our homes.

"Hey, Anna, how are you doing?" my Dad asked as I got home.

"Great, Dad," I said, smiling.

I just loved my Dad. He was always there to greet me when I got home from school. And he'd always have a snack waiting for me, and we'd chat and eat. Our talks didn't usually last long, but I just loved that part of the day. Plus, it was a great time to sneak in an unhealthy snack while mom was upstairs cleaning up.

"The Science Fair is coming up, and I don't know what I'm going to do this year," I told him. "Do you have any ideas?"

"Oh, no, I don't have any ideas. Remember, it was me who suggested the volcano a couple of years ago. But I know that you'll come up with something really great. I see you in your room all the time tinkering. Why don't you take one of those ideas and turn it into a science project," Dad suggested.

Dad was right; I did enjoy tinkering in my room. It all started with Mom getting me an inventor's box a few years ago. The box had all kinds of odds and ends in it, and Mom told me to let my imagination run wild. Every now and then, she'd replenish the box. On Saturdays, I started going to yard sales and buying old toys that I'd take apart and repurpose.

My inventions started out very simple at first, but the more I tinkered and tried different things, the more cool things I came up with. I learned to be more and more persistent. If an idea didn't work, I just tried something different until it did.

For Christmas gifts, I had even started making gifts for my cousins. They thought the toys I made were so cool. The last Christmas, I gave one of my little cousins a toy car that moved when you clapped. He became a clapping machine. He ran around the house all day clapping, grinning, and chasing that car.

But what did all of my tinkering have to do with a science project? Was what I was doing considered science? It must, if Dad and Joshua both suggested I turn my tinkering into a science project.

So, for the next five weeks, I tinkered. I sketched. I designed. I went through trial and error. Some things worked, but a lot of things didn't. But I kept trying.

Sometimes, I'd get really stuck, but then I'd just ask my Mom to take me to the library to find a couple of books. I'd get a new idea, and then I'd be off to tinker some more. I went through a LOT of trial and error, until finally, I had it, my Science Fair project.

I just hoped there would be a category I could enter it into.

Finally, the big day came, and I was super nervous. I walked up to the gym, rolling my wagon with the main part of my Science Fair project covered up inside of it. As I walked up to one of the judges, she asked me, "What category will you be entering your project into?"

"The engineering category," I said. I had done some research, and it turned out that people considered what I had been doing to be engineering.

Science Fair at East Creek Elementary School

"Engineering category. Let's see. Umm, I see chemistry, biology, botany, zoology, environmental sciences, physics, and even math, but no engineering," the judge said.

"But certainly, engineering is a science. It's a combination of science and math. Here, I'll add that category to the list. Go right over there and set up your project. I'll come by later with a sign that says engineering," the judge said as she smiled.

Propeller car

I breathed a sigh of relief. Not being able to enter the Science Fair after all of my hard work would have been worse than the volcano year. I gave my dad the thumb's up, and then he went outside to get the other pieces of the project that he had in the back of his truck.

I went over to the section of the gym the Judge pointed me to and began setting up my project. I was so excited to share with everyone what I had been working on for the last five weeks.

As Judges, parents, and other kids passed by, I began asking for volunteers to try out my project. I had created a mini roller coaster.

Propeller car

A 4th grader came by, and she had a look of awe on her face. "What's that?" she asked.

"It's a mini roller coaster. There's a button inside the cart. Just press it, and off you'll go. Wanna give it a try?" I asked her.

"Sure do!" she said.

So she climbed into the cart and fastened the seat belt I had made. When I said go, she pressed the button marked 'GO,' and off she went. The car slowly climbed a little hill, and then paused at the top. Then it made a sudden drop down the hill, and just as it did that, a camera snapped a picture of the girl. And, boy, it was a hilarious photo! The sudden fall had totally caught the girl off guard, which was just the reaction I had been hoping for.

Well, soon after that, more and more people began lining up to have their turns on the roller coaster. The principal even kept getting in line for a turn. The pictures of him coming down the roller coaster were super cool.

My Dad, Mom, and Joshua came walking over to me as the Science Fair was coming to an end. They all looked so excited. Joshua had several snapshots of himself making crazy faces as he'd ridden my roller coaster at least 5 times.

My Mom had a big gift box in her hands. "Anna, we are so proud of you. Even if you don't win, we are so proud of how hard you worked these last five weeks," she said.

First place gooooooes to you!

I opened the box, and it was full of the coolest tinkering items. I couldn't wait to get home to try to create something else. "Thanks, Mom," I said.

And just when I thought the day couldn't get any more exciting, the judge announced the winner while riding my roller coaster.

As she was about to drop down the hill, she yelled, "First place gooooooes to you!"

My tinkering had paid off!

Shenek Alston, a native of South Carolina, is a Christian, wife, and mother and lives in North Carolina. The Alstons have three children. Shenek feels that one of the most important things she will ever do is to homeschool her children, and wants to pour as much into them as possible. Shenek has a PhD in Statistics, and has taught Statistics at North Carolina State University. Currently, besides homeschooling her own children, she teaches online math classes for homeschoolers, and she also teaches Math at Art of Problem Solving Academy in NC. She also blogs about STEM activities for kids at www.makemathmorefun.com. Shenek hopes that Anna, Kid Engineer will inspire children to be creative, innovative, persistent, and to have fun tinkering! For more of Anna, Kid Engineer, check out www.annakidengineer.com.

Joyeeta Neogi is a freelance Illustrator. She has been working for over eight years with worldwide clients, creating high quality illustrations, mostly for Children's books using both traditional and digital medium in a colorful, playful style. She was born in Assam, India. She graduated in Fashion Design from Niift, India and worked as a Designer in the garment industry for over four years. After studying Graphic Arts and Illustration, she began her career as a freelance Children's book Illustrator. Her love for nature inspires the bright and colorful illustrations. Her style is a nice blend of realism and illustrated personality. She worked with Edcon publishing house, Om books, Sky Blue Bamboo, My Lap Shop Publishers, Partridge India, Counseling with HEART, Bookstand Publishing, Changefactor Limited, Kawa Kokoo, and Wow International. She currently resides in Bangalore, India with her techie husband and lovely creative daughter. You can see some of her illustrative work at https://www.behance.net/joyeeta_N or at https://joyeetaneogi.weebly.com/.

CPSIA information can be obtained
at www.ICGtesting.com
Printed in the USA
BVHW021909280422
635649BV00003BA/5